THE AMAZING MUMFORD

presents

THE MAGIC WEATHER SHOW

SHOW TODAY

MUMFIE

Featuring Jim Henson's Sesame Street Muppets

by Jocelyn Stevenson • Illustrated by Bill Davis

A SESAME STREET/GOLDEN PRESS BOOK
Published by Western Publishing Company, Inc.
in conjunction with Children's Television Workshop.

It was time for the magic show to begin. The curtain went up and The Amazing Mumford stepped forward.

"Welcome! Welcome! Welcome!" he cried. "Today my special magic show is all about weather!"

"Mumfie?" interrupted Grover. "I, Grover, your cute and adorable magician's assistant, would like to ask you a very important question. What is weather?"

"So glad you asked," said Mumford. "Weather is what it's like outside. Weather is sunshine, snow, wind, fog, and hail."

"Today, for my first trick," said Mumford, "I am going to make rain right here on stage! Are you ready?" Mumford turned to Grover.

Grover pulled an umbrella out of the magic chest. "Oh, yes, Mr. Mumfie. Grover is all ready for rain."

Mumford cleared his throat. "A LA PEANUT BUTTER SANDWICHES!" he said.

"Now, ladies and gentlemen," said Grover, "The Amazing Mumford will make nice, wet...

...SNOW! Brrrr!" Grover shivered.

"Oops," said Mumford. "I seem to have made a small mistake."

Grover opened the magic chest and pulled out a snow shovel. "Never mind," he said cheerfully. "Your trusty assistant will shovel the snow away before you can say 'jingle bells.'"

"Thank you, Grover," said Mumford. "Meanwhile,
I will try to make rain again."

The Amazing Mumford waved his wand over his head.
"A LA PEANUT BUTTER SANDWICHES!" he cried.

"Look, everybodee!" said Grover to the audience.
"Before your very eyes, The Amazing Mumford will make
a gentle, refreshing shower of . . .

...FOG! Oh, Mumfie!" called Grover. "Where are you? I cannot see a thing!"

CRASH! Grover banged into Mumford and they both fell with a thud to the floor.

"Nasty weather we're having," mumbled Mumford.

Grover crawled to the magic chest, pulled out a fog lantern, and turned it on.

"Ah, that is better," he said. "Now, Mumfie, I do not wish to seem impolite, but fog is not rain. Could you try again, please?"

RAIN DANCES for YOUNG and OLD

"Of course," said Mumford, dusting off his cape. "This time I will bring you rain or my name isn't The Amazing Mumford."

He carefully balanced his wand on the end of his nose. "A la peanut butter sandwiches!" he whispered.

"Ah-ha!" said Grover. "At last The Amazing Mumfie will bring you a torrent of..."

...WIND?"

A great wind swept across the stage, almost
blowing away Mumford and his brave assistant.

"HEY, MUMFIE!" screamed Grover through the howl
of the wind. "THIS IS NOT RAIN, IS IT?"

"NO! SORRY!" Mumfie screamed back.

"DO NOT WORRY!" yelled Grover, fighting against the wind to reach the magic chest. "I WILL FLY A KITE FOR THE AUDIENCE WHILE YOU TRY AGAIN!"

"THANKS!" shouted Mumford. He held onto his wand with both hands. "A LA PEANUT BUTTER SANDWICHES!"

The wind stopped.

"Whew, that is more like it," said Grover. "Now for some nice rain." No sooner had he said that than a large hailstone hit him — bonk! — on the head.

"Mumfie?" said Grover. "I do not think this is rain."

"I'm afraid you're right," Mumfie answered sadly. "This is . . . hail."

Grover dove for the magic chest and pulled out a hard
hat to cover his head. "Mumfie, please!" said Grover as
hailstones pinged off his hat. "I beg you. Get rid of this
hail. Try again for the rain."

"A LA PEANUT BUTTER SANDWICHES!" Mumford
yelled.

"O.K., everybodee!" Grover said to the audience. "This
time I am sure The Amazing Mumford will make buckets
and buckets of..."

…SUNSHINE!"

Mumford peeked out from under the table. "Well, it isn't rain," he said, "but it's better than my other mistakes."

"Yes, this is a nice change!" agreed Grover happily. "Why don't we forget the silly old rain and have a picnic?"

"Best idea I've heard all day," said Mumford.
"Look in the magic chest and see if we have
any peanut butter sandwiches."

The minute Mumford said "peanut butter sandwiches," the theater began to fill with clouds.

Grover looked up and sighed. "I wish you hadn't said that, Mumfie, because now it looks like it is finally going to...

...RAIN! Oh, my goodness!" said Grover.
"The Amazing Mumford has done it again!"